T.R. Bear

T.R.'s DAY OUT

T.R. Bear

T.R.'s DAY OUT

Terrance Dicks

Illustrated by
Susan Hellard

Piccadilly Press . London

046899
JS

Text Copyright © Terrance Dicks, 1985
Illustrations Copyright © Susan Hellard, 1985

Phototypeset by Area Graphics, Letchworth, Herts.
Printed and bound by Garden City Press Ltd.
Letchworth, Herts.
for Piccadilly Press, 1985,
64 Greenfield Gardens, London NW2 1HY

British Library Cataloguing in Publication Data
T.R.'s day out.—(T.R. Bear; 3)
I. Title   II. Hellard, Susan
823'.914[J]   PZ7

ISBN 0-946826-17-X

Other Titles in the Series
T.R. BEAR: ENTER T.R.
T.R. BEAR: T.R. GOES TO SCHOOL

Terrance Dicks is the producer for the BBC Classics series. He
is well-known for his children's books, principally for the
novelisations of *Dr Who*. Piccadilly Press publish his *Ask Oliver* series,
and *The Adventures of David and Goliath* series. He lives in the Hampstead area of London.

Susan Hellard is a popular young illustrator. She has illustrated a
number of books for Piccadilly Press, and is most noted for the
humorous insights in her illustrations. She lives in North London.

Chapter One

An Outing for T.R.

'You gotta take me, kid, you just gotta,' pleaded T.R. 'What are you trying to do, stunt my cultural development? I just gotta see that exhibition!'

It was a pretty unusual request to come from a teddy bear, thought Jimmy. But then, T.R. was a pretty unusual bear.

To begin with, he could talk. Not just pretend talk, the way lots of children do with their toys, but really talk.

T.R. could come to life.

As a matter of fact all toys can come to life, but they're not supposed to do it until their owners are safely asleep.

T.R. was inclined to break the rules when he felt like it.

Perhaps it was because he was an American bear, sent over in a parcel by Jimmy's Uncle Colin in the United States.

You could tell T.R. was different just by looking at him. For a start he wore a check hunting jacket, a bow tie and round wire spectacles with no glass. Instead of being round and cuddly, T.R. looked tough and determined.

T.R. was a bear who liked to get things done.

What he wanted to get done at the moment was to persuade Jimmy to take him with him on tomorrow's school trip to the British Museum. There was an American Exhibition on and T.R. was desperate to see it.

They were having their whispered conversation, or rather argument, in Jimmy's bedroom, just after bedtime.

The minute Jimmy's mum had come and kissed him goodnight and put the light out, T.R. had jumped down from the toy shelf on to Jimmy's bed, marched up to the pillow and started talking.

He had heard about the coming trip during the day – even when he wasn't talking, T.R. was always listening – and now he was determined to go along.

'Come on, kid,' he pleaded. 'Waddya say?'

'I say old chap, do stop making a pest of yourself,' drawled a superior-sounding voice.

It was Edward, Jimmy's other teddy bear, as British as T.R. was American. Once T.R. started talking the other toys usually joined in as well, as if they'd decided it was no use trying to keep their secret any longer.

'After all,' Edward went on, 'who wants to go to some boring old museum anyway?'

'That's not the right attitude,' said a

reproving female voice. 'A good museum is an educational experience. Even T.R. knows that. And if he's going, then I'm certainly going as well!'

Jimmy groaned into his pillow. You might think it was great fun having toys that came alive and talked to you, and of course in a lot of ways it was. The trouble was, his toys didn't just talk, they argued, not just with each other, but with him.

'Christopher Robin never had all this trouble with Winnie-the-Pooh,' thought Jimmy. 'All his toys ever did was stand round telling him how wonderful he was!'

The female voice came from the third toy in the room, a rag doll called Sally Ann that Jimmy had inherited from his sister Jenny. Sally Ann was a keen supporter of something she called 'Doll's Lib' which meant she was quite determined not to be put down, or left out just because she was 'only a doll'.

'Sure thing, Sally Ann,' said T.R. generously. 'Glad to have you along. You can be my guide, give me the tour.'

They were both taking it for granted they were going by now, thought Jimmy. No-one was asking *him*.

Jimmy sat up. 'Now wait a minute, you two. How am I supposed to explain taking a teddy bear and a rag doll on a trip to the British Museum? I can hardly say they want to improve their cultural development.'

'No problem, kid,' said T.R. briskly. 'Me and Sally Ann'll ride in that big old satchel of yours.'

'You won't see much from in there, will you?'

'Sure we will. We can just pop our heads out when no-one's around.'

'There won't *be* a time when no-one's around,' Jimmy pointed out. 'And if you two think I'm going to lug two talking toys around all day . . .'

'Three,' said Edward Bear's reproachful voice.

T.R. swung round. 'I thought you didn't want to come to some boring old museum?'

'Well, perhaps I was a shade hasty. I mean, you wouldn't leave a chap here all alone, would you?'

And so it was settled – somehow without any reference to Jimmy. They were *all* going.

And that was that!

*   *   *

'That looks like a pretty full satchel to me,' said Jimmy's brother George as Jimmy left the house next morning. 'What on earth have you got in there?'

'Oh, provisions – notebooks, stuff like that,' said Jimmy airily.

George gave him his older-brother type superior look. 'You're only going to the British Museum, you know, you're not exploring darkest Africa. Let's have a look.'

George made a grab for the satchel, but Jimmy snatched it away. 'You mind your own business,' he said, and slipped past George and out of the front door.

As he hurried along to school, Jimmy could hear a sort of muffled chorus coming from inside the satchel.

'I say, old chap, you might give a fellow a bit of room.'

That was Edward Bear.

Then a female voice. 'Come on, budge up a bit, T.R., there's a good chap.'

This was Sally Ann.

Then there came T.R.'s low rumble. 'Listen, lady, I've got your elbow in my ribs and Edward's foot in my ear. I'm the one who oughta be complaining.'

'You're the one who's taking up all the room,' grumbled Edward.

'That's right,' said Sally Ann. 'Some people are rather bulkier than others, you know!'

'Listen, nobody invited you two guys along. There's plenty of room back up on the toy shelf.'

By now the noise from the satchel was quite loud.

Suddenly Nick, one of Jimmy's school friends ran up to join him. 'What's all that noise coming from inside your satchel? Have you got a radio playing in there or something?'

Jimmy went red. 'Must have switched itself on by accident. You go on, Nick and I'll fix it.'

Nick ran ahead and Jimmy leaned down, opened his school bag and hissed, 'Now listen, you lot, shut up – or I'll stick this bag in the school cloakroom and leave it there all day.'

He ran on and caught up with Nick.

When they reached the school, the

mini-bus was standing in the playground with most of the class already inside.

Mr Briskin, Jimmy's teacher was running round and round like a dog chasing its tail. He was a thin, fair-haired young man, quite nice most of the time, but he was really too nervous and excitable to be a teacher. When things got too much for him, he sometimes got into a real tizzy.

He was in a tizzy now, because it was almost time for the mini-bus to leave and not everyone was inside yet. History had been Mr Briskin's subject at university, and he'd been preparing them for months for this visit.

When Jimmy and Nick appeared, he started jumping up and down with anxiety. 'There you are,' he squawked. 'Get in, get in, get in!' He stood in the doorway and looked round the bus. 'Now then, that's everyone, isn't it?'

Jimmy looked round too. 'Everyone except Timmy, Sir.'

Timmy was the smallest boy in the class, so small that everyone called him Mouse.

Mr Briskin exploded. 'I might have known it would be him. He's always late. Well, we shall have to go without him, we've got a very full timetable today, and I can't be expected to –'

Jimmy tugged at Mr Briskin's sleeve. 'Sir! *Sir!*'

Mr Briskin glared down at him. 'What is it, boy?'

Jimmy pointed. Mouse was standing at the door of the mini-bus, peering up at them through his glasses, too terrified to get on.

Mr Briskin gulped. 'All right, Timmy,' he said quite kindly. 'Don't just stand there, get on!'

Mouse scurried to a seat at the back of the mini-bus, Jimmy and Nick sat down together.

Mr Briskin looked round and took a final head-count – actually he took two, because he counted wrong first time. Finally he got it right and sat

down in the front, nodding to the
driver. They were on their way!

Chapter Two

The Fake

It was a short, but lively journey to the British Museum.

There was quite a bit of shouting and larking about from the class because they were excited, and quite a lot of yelling from Mr Briskin because he was even more anxious than usual.

Mr Briskin hated school trips, even more than he hated playground duty.

His idea of a teacher's life was standing in a classroom teaching a quiet well-behaved class, something which very seldom seemed to come his way.

The mini-bus driver seemed quite relieved by the time he pulled up on the pavement outside the British Museum and let them all out. He drove away, after faithfully promising to return at three o'clock to pick them up. The plan was that they should spend all day at the museum –

everyone had been told to bring a packed lunch and some money for refreshments.

Mr Briskin lined them all up.
'Right, everybody follow me. First
stop the Egyptians!' He paused,
looking round the class. 'Now
remember, the British Museum's a big
place, a *very* big place, very easy to get
lost in, and knowing you lot,
someone's almost certain to manage it.
Try and stay with the class, but if you
do get lost, just remember to be here,
outside the main entrance at three
o'clock, otherwise you'll have to find
your own way home!'

Then, like Napoleon at the head of
his troops, Mr Briskin led the class up
the steps and into the museum.

*   *   *

'Well, it's certainly big all right,' thought Jimmy as he stood with the others, staring around the cavernous entrance hall.

Perhaps because it was a weekday morning the museum wasn't very busy yet, and Mr Briskin and his class seemed lost in the huge echoing space.

But Mr Briskin was an old hand when it came to the museum. Confidently he led them up the stairs, along echoing corridors and into the main Egyptian Gallery.

'We'll start off with the funeral regalia,' he announced. 'When one of the Egyptian kings died it was customary to bury his treasure with him so he could make an impressive arrival into the other world . . .'

He led them past towering mummy cases towards a glass case filled with jewels and ornaments.

Jimmy was trailing along behind, since he didn't find dead Egyptians all that fascinating.

Suddenly, he heard a voice from inside his satchel. 'Get lost, kid!'

Jimmy looked down. 'No need to be rude, T.R.,' he whispered.

'I mean deliberately,' growled T.R. 'We're never going to get to see anything trailing round after this mob!'

Jimmy glanced at the others, all crowded dutifully around Mr Briskin, then edged backwards out of the door.

Once in the corridor he undid his school-bag. He looked round. For the moment the corridor was empty, 'All right, it's all clear,' he whispered.

Immediately T.R.'s head popped out of the bag, then Edward Bear's, then Sally Ann's.

'All right,' said Jimmy. 'Where now?'

Immediately, an argument broke out.

Edward wanted to see suits of armour and ancient weapons. 'Part of my British heritage, you know,' he said grandly.

Sally Ann called Edward a male chauvinist bear. 'I should like to see something rather more artistic. Greek statues, Etruscan vases, that sort of thing.'

T.R. let out a howl of protest. 'Listen you guys, let's not forget why we came here,' he growled. 'The special American Art Exhibition, remember?'

'T.R.'s right,' said Jimmy firmly. 'He was the one who wanted to come to the museum in the first place. You two will have to wait your turn.'

A museum attendant turned into the corridor, and immediately the three little heads disappeared inside the bag again.

Half-opening the bag, Jimmy went up to him and asked him the way to the American Exhibition, and the man began reeling off a long and complicated string of directions.

The American Exhibition turned out to be in a little side gallery at the end of a corridor on the far side of the museum.

A notice on a stand outside the gallery explained that it was a travelling exhibition, sponsored by the American government, and that it was due to spend a few weeks in all the different capitals of Europe.

At the moment the little gallery was completely empty.

Jimmy unfastened his school-bag and set it down on the floor. 'All right, you lot, now's your chance. You can get out and have a look round, while I keep watch in the doorway. If anyone comes I'll have time to give you a shout and you can nip back inside the bag again.'

T.R. was out of the bag and marching across the floor almost before Jimmy had finished speaking, and a little more cautiously Edward Bear and Sally Ann climbed out and followed him.

Jimmy stood by the door, keeping watch.

As it turned out, there was something for everyone in the American Exhibition.

Sally Ann found a display case full of the most beautiful American Indian embroidery, moccasins and pouches and clothes decorated with brightly coloured beads. She particularly liked the notice in the case, pointing out the importance of the squaws in preserving the tribe's artistic heritage.

Edward stood studying an exhibition rack of 'Guns that Won the West'. He pulled an imaginary cowboy hat down over his eyes and Jimmy guessed he was pretending himself as Buffalo Bill, or Billy the

Kid. As for T.R. there was only one exhibit in the gallery as far as he was concerned.

It was a painting, a full-length portrait hanging on the wall. It showed a rather tubby-looking little man sitting on a big white horse. He wore a vaguely cowboyish sort of outfit, there was a cartridge belt strapped round his waist, and he was carrying a rifle.

The man was staring ahead with a grim, determined look on his face, and he wore a pair of round spectacles.

T.R. marched straight up to the painting and stood staring up at it, an almost worshipful expression on his face. Somehow the man in the painting seemed to be staring straight back at him.

Jimmy went over and stood beside T.R. and for a moment they stood looking at the picture together.

Jimmy looked down at the fascinated T.R. 'Is that who I think it is?'

T.R. nodded, pointing to the notice beside the picture.

It read: 'Theodore Roosevelt, at the time he raised his famous troop of Rough Riders to fight in the Cuban War in 1898.'

'Yep,' said T.R. reverently. 'That was three years before he became President, of course.'

Jimmy knew that Theodore Roosevelt, Teddy for short, was T.R.'s great hero. Not surprisingly since according to T.R. all teddy bears were actually named after Teddy Roosevelt. Anyway, T.R. did his best to model himself on his hero, and even wore the same kind of round eye-glasses to be more like him.

Suddenly a voice boomed out behind them. 'Howdy there, little pardner!'

Jimmy swung round, horrified. He had forgotten to keep watch in the doorway, and now someone had come in – with the toys alive and moving about.

And what a someone!

The newcomer was small, but amazingly fat. He wore a flowered Hawaiian shirt ballooned out by his enormous belly, and there was a complicated-looking camera hanging round his neck. He wore cowboy boots and an enormous cowboy hat.

Jimmy glanced quickly downwards and saw that T.R. was lying flat on

his back, staring glassy-eyed at the ceiling, looking just like an ordinary toy.

Quickly, Jimmy bent down and snatched the little bear up. A quick glance round showed him that Sally Ann and Edward Bear were nowhere to be seen.

'Admiring good old Teddy Roosevelt, I see,' said the fat man. 'Gee, but he sure was some swell guy. Greatest President we ever had in the little old US of A.'

'I'm sure he was,' said Jimmy politely, and began backing away.

If he could pick up the other toys without the man noticing . . .

Tucking T.R. under his arm, Jimmy started edging towards the other end of the room.

Suddenly a voice from around his armpit muttered, 'Hold it, kid, there's something funny going on here. This guy's a fake!'

Chapter Three

Robbery!

The fat man swung round and glared suspiciously at Jimmy. 'What was that, pardner?'

'I didn't say anything!'

'Oh yes you did. Something about a fake.'

The man looked suddenly threatening, almost dangerous.

'Oh, I was just sort of thinking aloud,' said Jimmy hurriedly. 'Wondering if that painting could be a fake.'

The man shook his head. 'Oh, it's no fake, believe me. Matter of fact, it's a newly discovered portrait, been hidden away for years. It's worth a heck of a lot of money.'

'That's very interesting,' said Jimmy. 'Well, I must be going . . .'

T.R. was right, decided Jimmy, there was something very odd about this man. Perhaps he'd better wait outside and get the other toys later when the man had gone.

Clutching the now-silent T.R., Jimmy slipped out of the door.

As soon as they were out in the corridor, T.R. came to life again.

'We gotta stick around, kid,' he growled. 'That guy's as phoney as a three-dollar bill. If you ask me he's planning a heist.'

Jimmy stared at him. 'A what?'

'A robbery! That's it! He's planning to hi-jack Teddy Roosevelt's portrait!'

'He did say it was worth a lot of money,' said Jimmy thoughtfully. 'But what makes you so sure? He could be just an innocent tourist.'

T.R. shook his head. 'Not a chance. I tell you the guy's a fake.'

'How can you tell?'

'The way he talks, the way he's dressed.'

'Like an American tourist?'

Once again, T.R. shook his head. 'Like an Englishman's idea of an American tourist. The shirt, the hat, the boots, the camera, the accent – all together and all over the top.'

'Well, you ought to know, T.R. But if he is planning a crime he's made himself pretty noticeable. Anyway, what do we do now?'

'We sneak back in there. There's a display case just to the left of the door. If we duck behind that we can keep an eye on him.'

Jimmy hesitated and T.R. said, 'Look, we gotta go back in there sometime, Sally Ann and Edward are still inside. Oh, and put me down, willya?' As usual, once T.R. took charge, there didn't seem anything to do but obey.

T.R. slipped through the door, and seconds later Jimmy followed.

They both crouched behind the display case and peered cautiously out.

The fat man was standing in front of the Roosevelt portrait, studying it almost greedily.

He glanced quickly around the room, and Jimmy and T.R. ducked back, afraid he'd see them, but they must have moved just in time.

When they peeped out again, the fat man had gone back to studying the painting. Then he started to move.

He took off his cowboy hat, and then his cowboy boots, revealing ordinary white tennis shoes underneath.

He took off his gaudy Hawaiian shirt.

And then, to their amazement, he took off his stomach!

Suddenly the fat tourist had vanished, and in his place was a thin man in a black T-shirt, jeans and tennis shoes, someone you wouldn't look at twice.

Everyone would have noticed him coming in, thought Jimmy, but no-one would realise it was the same man going out.

The little man leaned over his removed 'stomach'. As they could now see, it was a sort of stomach-shaped bag, more or less like a rucksack, held on by straps and worn on the front instead of the back.

They watched fascinated as he took a number of objects out of the disguised container.

The first was a neatly printed notice. It read:

AMERICAN EXHIBITION
TEMPORARILY CLOSED

They ducked out of sight once again as the man hurried past their hiding place and popped outside, presumably to fix the notice on the stand outside the door. He then hurried back to the bag.

Next he took out a small metal black box with controls set in the lid. He glanced round the room until he located an electrical junction box in the far corner of the room. He hurried over to it and attached the black box. A light began flashing in its lid.

'A circuit-breaker to fix the

alarms,' whispered T.R. 'This guy's a real pro.'

Next the robber went up to the painting and lifted it carefully down from its hook, resting it against the wall. No alarm bells rang, so his black box gimmick must have been working.

The next thing to come out of the bag was a knife with a long thin blade.

'He's going to cut the painting out of the frame,' growled T.R. 'Gimme some kind of distraction, kid!'

Jimmy thought for a moment, fished a one-p coin out of his pocket and pitched it over the other side of the room.

It fell with a tiny clatter and the robber whirled round, staring at the area the sound had come from.

Seeing no-one was there he turned his attention back to the painting . . .

Suddenly Jimmy realised that T.R. was no longer beside him.

Looking round, he saw stealthy movement on the other side of the room. But it wasn't T.R.

It was Edward Bear and Sally Ann, creeping slowly towards the corner junction box.

The robber picked up his knife and moved forwards, preparing to cut the painting from its frame.

Just as the knife was about to touch the canvas a voice boomed, 'STOP!'

The robber leaped backwards in shock.

The voice seemed to be coming from the portrait itself.

On the other side of the room, Edward Bear and Sally Ann had just reached the junction box.

Unfortunately, it was just too high
on the wall for them to reach.

As Jimmy watched, Sally Ann
began climbing on Edward's
shoulders.

Nervously the thief approached the painting again.

As he reached out with his knife the voice boomed out again. 'You heard me! Keep your thieving hands away from my portrait!'

From the back of his white horse, Teddy Roosevelt seemed to glare accusingly at the man, who stared at the talking painting in utter amazement.

Jimmy grinned. There was only the tiniest space between the painting and the wall against which it was now leaning.

No room for a man to hide, or even a child. But plenty of room for a very small bear with a very big voice.

Springing forwards, the robber lifted the painting to one side.

There behind it stood T.R. Bear,

hands on hips and jaw stuck out, looking every bit as tough and determined as his famous namesake on the white horse.

'Beat it, you low-down, mangy rascal,' he roared. 'Before I call the cops.'

For a moment the robber stared at T.R. in amazement. Then as if in panic, he leaped forward, slashing with the knife.

T.R. ducked, and the robber raised his knife to strike again.

Balancing on Edward Bear's shoulders, Sally leaped up and grabbed the circuit-breaker, wrenching it free from the junction box. Sally Ann and Edward Bear fell to the ground, but the circuit-breaker came with them.

Suddenly the little gallery was filled

with the clanging of the alarm bell.

Now thoroughly panic stricken the thief ran for the door.

Jimmy decided it was time that *he* did something.

Dashing forwards, he threw himself on his hands and knees, sideways in front of the fleeing robber, who shot forwards over Jimmy's bent back and crashed to the ground.

Half-dazed he climbed to his feet and staggered forwards – straight into the arms of two brawny museum attendants who came rushing through the door.

The thief struggled furiously, and Jimmy used the distraction to grab T.R., Sally Ann and Edward and shove them back in his school-bag. 'Well done, kid,' whispered T.R. 'Teddy Roosevelt would have been proud of you. Now, let's get out of here!'

Chapter Four

T.R.'s Reward

As Jimmy headed for the door one of the struggling museum attendants called out, 'Hang on a minute, sonny. What's going on here?'

Jimmy paused in the doorway. 'Don't ask me. All I know is, I came in here to take a look at the exhibition and that chap dashed out and fell over me. Sorry, I must go now. I've lost the school party I'm with and I'll be for it if I don't find them again!

You can have all the credit.'

Before the museum attendant could say any more, Jimmy turned and ran. As he hurried along the corridor, Jimmy couldn't help laughing at the thought of the would-be robber's astonished face.

Still, he'd probably keep very quiet about what had really happened. Bad enough being captured by a kid. How much worse to have to admit to being captured by a kid, two teddies and a rag doll.

*　　　*　　　*

Jimmy arrived at the Egyptian room just as Mr Briskin and the rest of the class were leaving. 'Where on earth have you been, Jimmy?' demanded Mr Briskin. Luckily he didn't wait for an answer. 'Come

49

along now, we're just about to set off for the Etruscan gallery, then I thought we might look at some medieval arms and armour.'

'Be right with you, Sir,' said Jimmy cheerfully.

He was undoing his school-bag and sitting the three toys up inside so they'd have a good view of whatever was going on in the museum. Mr Briskin stared at him in astonishment. 'May I ask why you've brought those three toys with you, Jimmy?'

After such an eventful morning, Jimmy was past caring about whether anyone might think him crazy.

'I thought it might be educational for them, Sir. This lady is called Sally Ann, and this bear is Edward. I believe you've already met T.R.?'

'Yes, of course, how do you do?' said Mr Briskin, leaning forward to shake hands. He checked himself, suddenly realising he was having a conversation with a teddy bear – or trying to, anyway.

Edward Bear and Sally Ann and of course T.R. brought up the rear, peering out of Jimmy's school bag.

And they didn't miss a thing.

After all, everyone knows that teddy bears can't talk.

Can they?

All the same, thought Mr Briskin, there was something rather mysterious about that bear . . .

T.R. stared blandly at Mr Briskin.

Just for a moment, Mr Briskin could have sworn that T.R. *winked*. Absolutely impossible of course. It must have been just a trick of the light.

Mr Briskin drew a deep breath.

'This way, class,' he called, and led the expedition on its way.